THE FROCK UP

DOGG PACK SERIES

EVIE MITCHELL

THUNDER THIGHS PUBLISHING

ACKNOWLEDGEMENT OF COUNTRY

I acknowledge the Traditional Custodians of the lands on which I write, the Ngunnawal people, and pay my respect to elders both past and present.

I acknowledge the continued and deep spiritual relationship of the Australian Aboriginal and Torres Strait Islander peoples' to this land, and their unique cultural and spiritual relationships to the land, waters and seas and their rich contribution to society.

Always was, always will be.

To the man who rescued me from a faulty
zipper.
This book would never have happened if not
for you.

Also to my husband for laughing when I told
him this story.

And to Lucy.
Without you, my legs would be far colder, and
my heart far emptier.

THE FROCK UP

Millie

It started with a stuck zipper and ended with a man physically ripping me free of my dress.

Surprisingly, less hot than it sounds.

I'd been thanking my lucky stars that I'd never have to see him again—only to discover the dress-destroying-Good-Samaritan is my new billionaire boss.

Talk about a royal frock up.

Ash

When the woman I saved from a malfunctioning dress walks into my office, I'm sensing trouble.

She's tall, curvy, and ridiculously easy to fluster—all my weaknesses in one.

When I find myself daydreaming about her hamburger print underwear instead of my next invention, I *know* I'm in trouble.

Now I just have to convince her that our relationship could be... seamless.

Warning: This instalove goodness is inspired by the author's true-life run-in with a faulty zipper, her greedy reader FB group demanding this romance, and a guy who knows how to save the world. So, unzip and unwind as you enjoy this little slice of deliciousness!

CHAPTER 1

Millie

The dress was calling me.

I stared at the hot little number in the window of the far-too-expensive-for-my-taste boutique, my insides practically quivering with lust.

You could just try it on. Just see how it feels. You don't have to commit to anything.

The traitorous voice I liked to refer to as Millionaire Millie attempted to break down my willpower.

Unlike Millionaire Millie, I was not able to afford dresses worth hundreds if not thousands of dollars. Alas, being the co-owner of a struggling graphic design firm didn't get you far these days.

Just a little peek. I mean it's not often you find such wonderfully gorgeous dresses in your size.

I gave in, my hands pushing open the door to the store, my feet carrying me inside before I could even think to stop myself.

"Welcome to Alexa Ina Boutique, can I help you today?"

"I'd like to try on that one, please." I pointed at the gorgeous golden dress in the store window.

"Oh!" the saleswoman purred. "Great choice."

She found my size then led me down a short hall to a dressing room. n attractive man sat outside one of the stalls, a baby sleeping in a pram beside him. He had the kind of nerdy-but-cool looks I normally went for. He flipped through his phone not even bothering to glance up as we passed.

Why are all the good ones taken?

"Just in here."

She hung the dress carefully on a hook then shot me a grin. "I'll be right back. Call if you need anything."

As the door closed, I gazed in adoration at the gorgeous dress.

Just one little try. You don't have to purchase it. Just give it a little twirl.

The price tag had far too many zeroes for my budget but I shrugged off my fake designer dress and shimmied the figure-hugging frock up over my thick thighs, across my apple butt, and up my torso. I contorted myself in two, attempting to get the zipper up. It caught for a moment then pulled smoothly to the top, settling the material around my body with a loving embrace.

I twisted, staring at myself in the mirror.

Oh, yes.

The gorgeous gold fabric hugged all of my curves in a way that accentuated and flattered.

I look good. Really good.

I wanted nothing more than to live in this dress. I wanted to wear this dress to a red-carpet premiere and Sunday dinner. I wanted to sleep in this dress.

For the price you'd be paying for it you'd need to.

With a heavy sigh, I gave one last twirl, giggling as the light danced off the beading.

Alright Millie, back to reality.

With another sigh, I reached for the zipper, frowning as it caught just above my hips.

I twisted, looking over my shoulder to see if the material had caught in the teeth.

I couldn't see anything, so reached for the tab again, giving it a hard yank.

No movement.

Okay, this is weird.

I pulled at the material, trying to work the zippered prison down my body, wincing when I heard the seams groan in protest as I pulled it up and over my butt. With a shimmy, I attempted to get it past my hips to no avail.

Shit. Shit. Shit. Shit!

"How does it look?" The saleswoman asked, giving my door a light knock.

"Ah, wonderful. But I seem to have... that is...." I swallowed, my palms beginning to sweat. "I think the zipper is stuck."

"Oh, that happens sometimes. Can I come in and help?"

I yanked the skirt back down, hiding my underwear.

"Okay."

I opened the door and she slipped through, the guy on the other side still glued to his phone.

Must be an engrossing game.

The sales assistant gave the zipper a tug, letting out a surprised huff when it didn't budge.

"Hmm, just a moment." She stuck her head out the door, calling, "Gwen, can you come in here please?"

My cheeks flushed as Gwen joined us in the tiny stall.

"Oh, this happens all the time," she assured me, taking a firm grip on the zipper. "Ready? One, two—" She yanked down, the fabric protesting as the zipper remained fixed in place.

"Oh."

Oh? Oh!? What does 'Oh' mean?

"Is... is everything okay back there?" I asked, anxious butterflies now taking flight in my belly.

"Ah, it seems the zipper has broken. Not your fault, looks like a fault with the dress. Let's take this off another way." With a rough yank, she attempted to pull the dress up, managing to send me tripping into the mirror with a yelp.

"Ah, I see the problem," she said with a shake of her head. "Your derriere is disproportionate to your hips. Perfect for this dress, not so great for being stuck in it."

A quick glance in the mirror revealed the material was now bunched at my hips, my novelty print underwear on full show.

This is my punishment for listening to Millionaire Millie—abject mortification.

"Look, how about I just buy this one—" I began, horrified at the idea of anyone seeing more of my body.

"Don't fret, we'll get you out."

Gwen reached for the top of the dress, giving it a sharp pull, the material falling to pool around my waist. Now both my top and bottom half were on show—displaying my hamburger underwear and Pokémon bra.

So, this is hell. I always wondered what it would be like. Turns out it's having your wildest dream of living in your favourite dress fulfilled in the worst possible way.

With a shake of her head, Gwen tapped a finger against her lips.

"I think we'll need to cut it."

"I'm sorry, did you say—" I leaped back as she pulled a Stanley knife from her pocket. "What are you doing!?"

She gestured at the knife. "Cutting you out."

"Abso-fucking-lutely not!" I squealed, pressing into the back of the stall. "I will *live* in this dress for the rest of my life before I allow you to bring that knife anywhere close to my skin!"

"But—"

"Excuse me," a male voice sounded from the other side of the stall door. "I can't help but overhear."

I closed my eyes, the heat of my blush enough to give me a sunburn.

Please God, take me now.

He pushed the door open, and I was *mortified* to realize that the guy who'd been playing on his phone was no mere mortal.

No, he looked like a Greek god. Tall, dark, stunning green eyes, a flop of dark hair—a nerdy dreamboat in my shipwreck of a life.

I don't know what I did to accrue this kind of karma but it must have been hella bad for this to happen.

"May I be of assistance?"

My soul, which had already made peace with the fact I was going to be buried in this dress, scoffed.

And what exactly can you do, Mr. Attractive? Whip out some WD-40? Perhaps you have a spare stick of butter in your back pocket? Some olive oil in your kid's pram?

He reached out, his hands settling on my hips as he turned me, gently smoothing a small amount of the material. I felt his hands fist the fabric just above the zipper, his skin warm on my back.

I twisted my neck, looking over my shoulder. "What are you—"

With a rough yank, he ripped the zipper apart, the material parting as if he were Moses and it the Red Sea.

"How did you...?"

He grinned, reaching up to brush hair from his forehead. "Not the first time I've been involved in a zipper-related rescue."

"I... thank you."

He winked. "Don't mention it. I'm Ash by the way."

"Hi, I'm—"

The baby began to cry outside the stall.

"Shit, sorry. I'm on baby-watching duty. Nice to meet you, zipper girl."

He stepped out of the stall, leaving me with the gaping sales assistants.

Gwen shook off her shock first.

"So, can I ring this up for you?" she asked, touching the material I'd clutched to my chest.

"You mean the prison dress?"

She nodded, her face earnest.

For once, Millionaire Millie and I were in perfect agreement.

"No."

CHAPTER 2

Ash

Being a billionaire sucked.

I pinched the bridge of my nose barely suppressing a frustrated sigh.

"Ash?" James, my brother and the Chief Financial Officer for our company, turned to look at me. "Thoughts?"

I hate it. It should never have seen the light of day.

I cleared my throat, softening my reaction. "It doesn't have any connection to our brand."

The mock-ups were for a new company logo. Now that we were only months away from floating on the Federal Exchange, our media team had suggested we unveil a new logo. Considering the current logo was just our name with a line underneath it, I could see why we might want to explore alternatives.

Didn't make this process any easier though. *Who knew graphics were so hard?*

"Can you explain what's wrong with it?" Sally, the head of my PR branch, asked, her tone overly patronising.

Sally regularly acted as if I were a naughty schoolboy given too much candy. She was good at her job, but damn if I didn't hate every moment of our conversations.

Last time I ever employ a head of division without meeting them.

"Everything." I gestured at the logo that proudly took up the majority of the giant screen. "I know you think it looks like two trees but all I see are two people engaging in... you-know-what."

All heads swivelled towards the screen, silence descending.

"Oh, they're fucking," James said, his voice choked with laughter. "Well damn."

"Ah...." Sally cleared her throat, a faint flush working its way up her neck. "We'll fix it."

"Who did we have on this one?" I asked, glancing at the clock on the wall.

Only twenty minutes until I can get out of here.

"It was Ronald Media."

I rolled my eyes. "So, another big-name company?"

Sally's face took on a pinched look. "Yes, sir."

"Ash," I corrected her for the millionth time. "Fire them. If they didn't realise they were producing pornography, then I don't trust them with my brand." I stood, tucking my hands into my pockets. "We done?"

"No, we're not." Sally gestured at the logo. "This is the last major company willing to work with us. You've fired the rest. You're too exacting. You need to meet us halfway."

The room went electric as I stared at her.

"Sally, this company was founded on three principles—the core of which is that we don't compromise." I looked pointedly at the screen. "I'm not meeting anyone halfway on junk like that."

"There's no one else! None of the big firms will work with us."

"Then find a small business." I looked pointedly at the logo. "The last three launches have been by big corps who have screwed it up. Does no one else remember the plastic issue at the cell launch?"

There were winces around the table.

"We need to get this right." I gestured at the room. "This all started because James and I took a gamble. We were small but determined. Let's get back to our roots. Let's give someone else the same opportunity we had."

Sally closed her eyes, sucking in a long breath. "And who would you suggest? Do I just pluck someone from the phonebook?"

I pulled my phone from my pocket, searching for graphic designers in the local area. "Here, there's a list right there." I handed her the phone. "Pick the top recommended, set them a task—say like designing a logo for the new water filters we're rolling out next month— and I'll pick one from there."

"Sir, this is—"

"Ash," I said, suddenly weary of this conversation. "It's just Ash."

Sally pressed her lips together, her face pinching. "Ash, we need you to choose by the end of the month if we're going to organise the launch ahead of the float. Can you do that?"

I shoved my hands into my pockets, giving her a sharp nod. "I promise to agree to something by the end of the month." I looked meaningfully at the fellatio trees still on the screen. "So long as it's not another like that." I turned back to the table. "Is that all?"

James nodded, rising from his seat, one hand buttoning his suit jacket. "I think we can take it from here. Will you be in the lab?"

I shook my head. "My office. I need to fix the issue with the intake for the engine."

James nodded. "I'll have lunch sent in."

With one last look at the board room, I turned on my heel, heading for my office.

Seven years ago, this business had just been me, James, and some seed money from our former foster brother, Jay. Now we were in four countries, a billion-dollar company, and talking acquisitions while serving caviar at bullshit functions where people who wouldn't let us in the door fawned over us, desperate to lick our shoes.

Maybe James enjoyed it, but I didn't. All I wanted was more time to create. If I could, I'd leave all this shit to the suits we hired. But James wanted me to be hands-on, and today's presentation reminded me of how important it was to have my finger on the pulse.

In the hall, I passed employees who offered me greetings as they did God only knew what, their faces blurring together until I couldn't tell one from the other.

I used to know everyone by name. Used to know their birthday, their partner, their kids. Now, I don't have a fucking clue.

My chief of staff, Dylan, looked up, sending me a grin. "I take it Sally was a nightmare?" They asked, watching me stalk towards my office.

"When isn't she? Who hired her?"

"I believe it was Hazel. She said it would be good for the company to have an older influence."

"Remind me to forget to cut her a Christmas bonus."

Dylan laughed, following me into my office. "What do you need?"

"Quiet. I need this afternoon to get this intake issue sorted."

They nodded. "Got it. I'll bar the door and breathe fire on anyone who attempts to enter."

"Thanks, Dyl." I settled at my desk. "Oh, and you're still on for beers at Yaluna tonight, right?"

They nodded. "Of course. All those delicious executives just waiting to sweep little old me off my feet?" They grinned. "Bring it on."

I rolled my eyes. "It's a work thing, Dyl. Something, something, new potential contract, remember?"

"Doesn't mean I can't look." Dylan sent me a wink and then backed out of the office, shutting the door firmly behind them.

Finally alone, I leaned back in my chair,

loosening my collar as I breathed freely for the first time all morning.

Who would have thought I'd hate being the boss?

Determined to sort out the intake issue with our prototype engine, I began to draw on my pad, losing myself in the familiar flow of curves and lines as I sketched out the biggest problem I was facing—finding the woman whose underwear haunted my dreams.

Wait. What?

I sat back, staring at the face on my sketch pad.

It's burger babe.

I'd drawn her gorgeous face from memory, surprised that I'd noticed the beauty mark at her temple and the fly-away hair that tickled the curve of her cheek.

I'd nicknamed the woman from the dress store burger babe in honour of her underwear. I was still kicking myself that she'd left before I'd got her number. But it was Kat, my sister-in-law's birthday, and the shopping trip and lunch was her first major outing with my newest nephew. While I'd been happy to celebrate, I also had an ulterior motive—convincing her I'm the best choice for godfather. It had become something of a competition between my brothers and me.

Burger babe's face stared up at me, hauntingly stunning. Something moved in me, an almost aching yearn that began radiating in my gut, setting my teeth on edge.

Well, damn.

I hadn't been this distracted since... since...

Never.

I ran my fingers through my hair, staring at the rough sketch.

"Well fuck. What do I do now?"

CHAPTER 3

Ash

"This is a terrible idea."

"It's not," I said, grinning at my sister-in-law. "It's a great idea."

Kat raised an eyebrow. "It's not. It's very creepy."

"Psh." I waved a hand in her direction. "It's romantic."

Hayden—my eldest brother and Kat's husband—shook his head. "I have to agree with my wife. It's creepy as fuck."

I made a face. "You're the kind of guy who thinks cleaning up poop is a romantic date. I'm not sure you get a say."

Hayden tossed a pillow my way. "Once!

And it was part of the town's efforts to improve the local dog park."

"You still made me clean up poo and called it a date," Kat said with a grin. "You're lucky I still love you."

A wet sound came from Lewis, the baby letting out a little sigh.

"Speaking of poo." Kat kissed his cheek and then handed him to Hayden. "Your turn Daddy."

Hayden grinned, carrying Lewis down the hall, his voice carrying as he praised his son for his bowel movements.

"Is he congratulating Lewis on a poop?" I asked, baffled by my brother.

"Yeah, don't ask. Just go with it." Kat rolled her eyes. "You should see how he is with the other kids. He showers them with constant praise. I worry for their future."

We exchanged a laugh as Hayden's voice floated down the hallway. "I heard that!"

Kat sobered; her gaze sharp as she considered me.

"What?" I asked, feeling suddenly exposed.

She tilted her head to one side. "You're different, Ash. You've returned to the Cove different."

Yeah well, a billion dollars and a trillion responsibilities will do that to you.

"I'm seven years older."

"Not to mention a billion dollars richer," she said with a grin.

"Yeah." I shrugged, that strange yearning feeling crawling under my skin.

"Why'd you come back to the Cove? Why not stay in Silicon Valley?"

Straight to the point.

Capricorn Cove wasn't the kind of place most people thought of when someone said 'billionaire'. But between the tax cuts the Kingdom of Astipia was offering investors, and the fact our small town was perfectly positioned between two major cities—close enough to commute each day, it was a no-brainer.

And that didn't even account for the fact I'd missed my family. Seven years in another country was long enough. I missed them and the breathing space they afforded me.

I'd grown up here, adopted by Will Dogg when I was only five years old. My best memories were of this town—surfing on the weekends, parties on the beach, and driving up to Widows Peak during the winters to snowboard. My family was here. All six brothers and one sister—none of whom I was related to by blood.

At the older end of the family tree there

was Hayden, at thirty-five he was the most established of our brood with his own house and veterinary practice. He'd been married to Kat for seven years and they had three kids—Laura, Lenny, and Lewis.

Then came the ones that were out of home —James at twenty-seven, me at twenty-five, and Ryan at twenty-one. Still living with Dad and his wife, Karen, was Sam at sixteen and Janeane at seven.

My phone buzzed, my brother's ring tone obnoxiously loud as it blared Timber by Pitbull and Ke$ha.

Speak of the devil and he shall appear.

Kat chuckled. "Is that Jay's ringtone?"

I sighed, closing my eyes. "Yep."

And there was Jay—the one brother who'd aged out of the system before Dad could adopt him. The thirty-three-year-old may be a Wood in name, but he was Dogg at heart.

I slid my fingers across the screen, accepting his call.

"Jay, when did you change my ringtone?"

"Last night, listen. I need you to babysit for me. I need to take my girl out. We're a bit desperate."

I flicked a glance at Kat. "Isn't that what a godparent is for?"

"Oh, shut it. You know you're first preference for the next kid."

Between my two married brothers, I had three nephews and one niece—for none of whom I was a godparent.

"Next kid? Something you're not telling me, Woody?"

Jay barked out a laugh. "Considering we've only just been cleared for sex after Rohan's birth, I'd say it's a bit premature. But look after Rohan for a few hours tonight and I might be able to deliver on that baby sooner than later."

I made a face. "TMI, dude."

"Please, Ash? My girl needs a decent sleep and she's not gonna do that if I don't force her."

"Of course, bring Ro over. The nursery is all setup."

"Thanks, bro. We'll be over after his feed. He'll go right down for a few hours. Piece of cake after that."

Having met Rohan, I knew that wasn't even remotely true. But I loved my nephew fiercely and didn't mind losing my hearing for a few hours. "See you soon."

I hung up, finding Kat watching me. "What?"

She grinned. "You want a family, Ash. It's obvious."

Her words stirred up the longing in me.

"Well, yeah. Of course. Doesn't everyone?"

She shook her head. "No. And that's okay. It's just that you're young to be—"

I groaned, pressing a hand to my face. "Not you too."

"What? I'm only telling the truth."

"Twenty-five isn't young." I felt ancient inside, dried up.

Kat pursed her lips together, dropping the subject. "Why burger babe?"

I hesitated, looking down at the drawing that lay between us. "I don't know."

Liar.

I knew exactly why I wanted her—she hadn't known who I was. And in a world where I couldn't go five steps without someone wanting something from me, it felt good to be ordinary.

Kat sighed. "Fine. Publish the post."

I raised my eyebrow. "Really?"

She nodded; her expression resigned. "Who knows? Maybe it will actually work."

I grinned. "Oh, it's gonna work."

It had to.

CHAPTER 4

Millie

"**M**illie?"

I looked up from where I was pouring over our accounts, desperate to find enough money in the budget to keep our little business ticking along for the next quarter.

It's not looking good.

"Yeah?" I asked, rubbing my eyes. "What's up, Keiko?"

My friend and art director held up her phone. "Have you seen this email?"

I shook my head, gesturing at the papers spread across my desk. "This is my life right now."

"Babe, look at your email. *Now.*"

Her tone had my eyebrows raising. "Is it a job?"

"Millie—email. Now."

I twisted, turning to my computer, quickly navigating to my virtually empty inbox. My stomach pinched at the lack of interest from prospective clients.

You knew going in this would be a struggle.

After all, who started a design business in a small town like Capricorn Cove? No one. And for good reason.

The email in question was from Dogg Wood Industries.

"Dogg Wood Industries?" I asked, clicking on it. "Do we know them?"

"Read it."

My eyebrows rose as I read the request, something like hope beginning to unfurl in my belly.

"Holy shit."

The organisation wanted us to bid to develop a full launch campaign for a new fully recyclable water filter

"Holy shit, Kei. This is...." I trailed off, unable to complete my thought.

Kei nodded, her dark hair bobbing in time to her movement. "Right? Millie, this could be huge for us."

"But why us?" I looked up, a horrible

thought crossing my mind. "Shit, do you think we're being catfished? Is this legit?"

I quickly googled the company's name, blinking as their logo appeared on the screen. "Oh, wow. That's horrible."

Keiko came around my desk, wincing at the image on the screen. "Mm, they definitely need our help."

She leaned over my shoulder, her familiar lemongrass perfume tinting the air. "Look at the email." She tapped a finger on my screen. "It's the same address as the email."

A flock of pterodactyls took flight in my belly, my body growing damp. "Shit. This is real."

Keiko squeezed my shoulder. "Yeah, it is. This is our chance, babe. We could take this company to the next level."

"You mean meeting our monthly payments?"

She grinned. "I mean growing to domestic. No longer relying on local businesses. No more fighting for every little scrap. If we land this, they might even be interested in a retainer. This could be huge for us."

I looked around my little office, attempting to calm my mind.

"Well, we better get to work. We have a pitch meeting next week."

CHAPTER 5

My phone was blowing up.

Journalists, friends, and family were all trying to reach me—none so desperately as Sally, who'd threatened Dylan with bodily harm to get an appointment with me.

"What—" she started, her tone glacial. "—did you think you were doing?"

I shrugged, feeling a little like a kid with his hand caught in the cookie jar. "Trying to find a missed connection."

"Do you have any idea how much damage this could have done? You're not a regular twenty-year-old, Ash. You're a CEO! You need to act like it."

I'd tweeted about the missed connection—three little lines. Nothing crazy.

Apparently, as romantic gestures went, this was a doozy. The media had latched on to the story and were frothing to find the mystery woman. I'd been told by a good friend in retail that sales in burger print clothing had jumped through the roof overnight.

"I know I'm not normal, Sally."

But for once, I want to be.

Burger babe had ruined me. I'd found myself back in the boutique, staring at the dress that had started this whole mess, imagining I could still catch the scent of her perfume in the air.

I mean, I'm pathetic, but it's sadly romantic at the same time. How very gothic of me.

"Then why did you do it?"

Because I can't get her out of my head.

I blew out a breath. "I don't know. I guess I forgot for a second."

"Forgot?"

I shrugged. "It happens."

She seemed to be struggling to suppress whatever words were burning on the tip of her tongue.

Go on, Sally. Let me have it.

"You're not a child, Ash. You are a grown man. You are a CEO. *The* CEO. You founded this company and have grown it to be what it is today. But that growth—that exponential growth that has allowed you the luxuries you have today—it relies on you maintaining it. You have employees who need you to lead."

I sucked in a breath, feeling as if I'd been punched in the gut. "Noted."

"Now." She shifted in her chair, reaching down to pull a tablet from her bag. "Let's talk design agencies. I approached eight small-to-medium-sized businesses that had stellar reviews. Of these, five agreed to submit a proposal. Of those five, only three are suitable. I've assembled the package for you to approve."

She tapped on her screen, casting the three logos onto the monitor on one of the walls in my office.

Of the three, one stood out.

"The bottom one. What's their pitch?"

She hesitated, her finger hovering over the screen. "The logo is good, but the launch pitch.... It's quite ambitious."

"Play it."

The video rolled, the sounds of nature filling my office, overlaid by an instrumental medley. Short snippets of people from around the world played across the screen—a man sweating as he ran up a hill track beside a clear flowing stream, a woman and her daughter swimming, and a couple crying as they broke up on the beach. Each focused on the water in the scene.

The music shifted, the images changing to sludge-filled water, dark and horrible. To water contaminated by pollutants.

It cut to a young girl holding one of our water filters. As she poured filthy water through the filter, clear water emerged, filling the glass.

The final image was of the clear glass. Words appeared on the screen.

Every drop counts.

"Wow," I said as the screen faded to black. "That was exceptional. What's the ambitious part?"

"They want Dogg Wood Industries to partner with a not-for-profit whose aim is to bring clean and safe drinking water to everyone. They want us to donate two filters for every one sold."

"Sally, this is perfect. This is exactly what we were aiming for when we created this product."

Her lips pursed together in a way I'd begun to recognise as a signal of her displeasure.

I sighed. "Go on."

"Accounts did the sums. We'll lose money for the first five years."

"How much?"

"At least ten percent."

I leaned back in my seat, pressing a button on my phone.

My brother answered immediately. "Yo, bro, what's up?"

"James, if we lost ten percent on the water filtration over five years, what are we looking at figure-wise?"

There was a pause. My brother was a certified genius when it came to numbers—hence becoming my chief financial officer.

"About eight-to-ten million, depending on sales."

"And if it's because we actively donate to charity?"

"Dude," he said, sounding amused. "You know any donations are a tax write-off. I'd be throwing more at it. Ten percent? Move it to fifty."

"Thanks."

I hung up, turning to look at Sally. "Let's book this agency."

She sucked in a breath. "Are you sure?"

I looked back at the screen. "Yeah. Let's do it."

CHAPTER 6

Millie

I smoothed my skirt down, my palms sweaty as fuck. Beside me, Keiko stared straight ahead, her expression neutral.

"You good?" I asked, my voice barely above a whisper.

"I'm shitting myself and trying not to look like I am. So, no."

I grinned. "Well, at least we look like we belong."

Mai, Keiko's sister, was a seamstress for a local dress boutique. She dabbled in her own fashion design, specialising in eco-friendly clothing. When we'd mentioned the campaign to her, she'd practically orgasmed, demanding to make us a suite of corporate wear.

"Dogg Wood Industries is legendary in the eco-space," she'd told us as she'd taken our measurements. "Ash Dogg built the first green battery—every part of it can be recycled or breaks down to compost. The company prides itself on being carbon neutral and improving the environment. Did you know the CEO and CFO purchased tracks of land in Capricorn Cove just to stop developers?"

I hadn't known, but now I did. And it scared the shit out of me.

Please let this go well. Please, please, PLEASE!

"Ms. Hawthorn? Ms. Sakamoto? I'm Sally Turner, head of public relations. Mr. Dogg will see you now."

I swallowed, exchanging a terrified look with Keiko as the stern-looking woman led us through the offices.

"Nice place you've got here," Keiko said as we passed open-plan desk spaces decorated in a variety of colours.

"Mr. Dogg believes in friendly competition. Each work area and team are invited to create their own names and symbols. He believes it makes them more cohesive."

"That's really cool. What's your team called?"

Sally glanced at me, her expression frosty. "We don't have a name."

Over her head, Keiko sent me wide eyes. *Well, she seems like a barrel of fun.*

"We're here."

She pushed open the door to the meeting room, revealing a square table at which sat four people—two men and two women.

I stumbled to a halt as my gaze caught on the man sitting at the far side of the table, his expression as equally as stunned as mine.

"It's—"

"—you!"

I stared at him as he pushed to a stand, my face flaming.

"You know each other?" Sally asked, her eyes narrowing in on me.

"No—"

"Not quite—"

"—that is—"

"—what I mean to say is—"

We both stopped, nervous giggles bursting free.

"Let me start over." I thrust out my hand to the nerdy-hot guy. "I'm Millie Hawthorn."

"Ash Dogg."

I froze, my body stiffening. "I'm sorry, did you say Ash *Dogg*?"

He nodded, his grin quick. "Yeah."

"As in *the* Ash Dogg?"

He nodded again, his grin widening.

Oh, shit.

Keiko nudged me, her elbow not at all subtle.

"Sorry, this is my business partner and art director, Keiko Sakamoto."

"Nice to meet you."

I watched as he shook Kei's hand.

"Should we get started?" Sally asked, her expression still suspicious.

"Sure."

We took seats at the table and were introduced to Ash's brother, James Dogg, his executive assistant Hazel Green, and Ash's executive assistant, Dylan Witcherson.

I noticed that everyone in the room except Sally wore a small lapel pin which read *Please use pronouns* with their preferred pronouns printed on the pin.

That's a great idea. I should organise some for our people.

I glanced up, finding Sally's gaze on me.

Maybe after I find out if we've landed the account.

"Your pitch was impressive," James started, leaning forward in his seat. He looked nothing like his brother, his body big and thick. He looked less like a CFO and more like a boxer awaiting his time in the ring.

"Thank you. We were actually inspired by the product." Keiko gestured at me. "Millie's extended family is from Mourinada in the South Island. You might remember a few years ago, they experienced a water crisis when some toxic waste was accidentally disposed of in the local water catchment. Water safety is a passion close to her heart."

I nodded. "This campaign has the ability to change lives. We'd love to be a part of this movement."

James shot his brother a grin. "Well, Ash? It's your baby."

I glanced at the CEO, finding his gaze on me.

"I loved it. We're going ahead with *Every drop counts*."

Keiko shot me a triumphant grin.

"But that's not what we're here to talk about today." Ash leaned in, his expression serious as he stared at me. "Millie, how do you feel about our current logo?" He nodded at the print on the back of the door.

I hesitated, wondering if this was a test. "Um... it's... basic." I scrambled for something positive to say. "The line is very... blue."

The table chuckled.

"You hate it."

I crumbled in the face of Ash's amusement. "Yeah, I really do."

"Good." He slid a folder across the table. "We're looking for a new logo. We want it to better represent our brand. If you're willing, we'd love to offer Thorn and Kei Designs this project."

Joy and abject terror warred in my gut.

This is everything we've ever wanted. Oh, God. What if we fail?

Ash watched me with those knowing green eyes, his expression reassuring.

"We loved everything you guys did with the water filters. We believe you'll do the same with our logo."

I swallowed, glancing over at Keiko, her face as equally stunned as mine.

"We'll do it," I said, reaching for the file. "Thank you."

Ash grinned, his body relaxing. "Great. I can't wait to get started."

CHAPTER 7

Ash

I watched through the glass as Millie chatted to Dylan, setting up a time to meet with me tomorrow.

Anticipation simmered under my skin; my gaze greedy as I watched her.

Tomorrow isn't soon enough.

An image of her superimposed itself across my vision. I could see my hands as they fisted the material of her stuck dress. I could feel the material giving way under my effort, exposing her to me.

Fuck this.

I turned, checking the calendar of meetings Dylan religiously left on my desk.

Three meetings and a call to Tokyo. Fuck.

The three meetings were about the new engine, but I was still working on the intake issue so the updates would be minor.

What's the point of being the boss if you can't move shit around?

There were only three meetings I'd ever blown off in my life—two as a result of a stomach flu that had left me worshipping the toilet, and one because the guy had refused to acknowledge Dylan and Hazel in the meeting. I didn't deal with douchebags.

I pressed a button, buzzing Dylan.

"What's up, boss?"

"Dyl, can you cancel my meetings? Except Tokyo. I'll take that at home."

There was a long pause. "Um, sure. You feeling okay?"

"Peachy." I watched as Millie pressed the button for the elevator, shooting her partner a large grin. "I just have something I need to do."

I caught the women in the lobby, my private elevator quicker than theirs.

"Hey," I greeted, falling into step beside them. "Fancy meeting you here."

Millie's face flushed a deep crimson. "Mr. Dogg. Hello again, I—"

"Just Ash," I corrected. "Everyone calls me Ash."

She bit her lip, exchanging a glance with Keiko. "Right, sorry. Ash, of course."

"Are you both headed back to the Cove?"

"Millie is," Keiko said with a grin. "But I'm meeting some friends for a drink."

I nodded, pausing to hold the door open for them. "Did you drive?"

"Keiko did. I was going to catch a bus back."

I gestured at the private car idling at the curb. "Why don't you come with me?"

I caught Millie's arm, steadying her as she tripped.

"Oh, oh no. I couldn't. That would be such an imposition. Definitely—"

"Come on. Seems silly when we're both going the same way."

"But—"

Keiko gave her a little push. "Go! It'd be faster than the bus. And maybe Ash can give you a better feel for the company? Give us a bit of a jump start on the design?"

That little gem landed with Millie; I could see it in the way she hesitated.

"I'm all yours until six," I told her with a grin. "Should I start with the story of how we started the company in my bedroom or the story of the time we burnt down my dad's garage?"

Keiko grinned, shooting me a knowing look. "Have a lovely night, Ash. And thanks again for this opportunity."

She stepped into the bustling crowd, quickly being swept away. Millie hesitated; her expression flustered.

"Are you absolutely sure I won't be imposing?"

"Positive," I confirmed.

"Well... okay."

My mind exploded in triumphant celebration as I fought to keep my expression pleasant.

"After you."

We slid into the backseat of the car, the driver closing the door behind us.

"Is this electric?" she asked, running her hands over the smooth leather of the electric car as we pulled away from the curb.

"Yeah. All the execs get one, and we give a financing option to any staff member who wants to purchase."

She glanced up at me from underneath her bangs. "You're really passionate about the environment."

I cleared my throat, unsure of what to say.

"My dad owns a lumber yard. Sounds like

an oxymoron to say he's one of the most sustainably-minded guys around, but it's true. He's never cut down old wood forests—and fought tooth and nail to ensure that reserves in Capricorn Cove are protected."

"You just purchased a bunch of land for that reason, right?"

I grinned, shooting her a raised eyebrow. "Checking up on me?"

She flushed, her fingers tangling in the strap of her bag. "N-n-no. Mai, Keiko's sister. She's studying to be a fashion designer but wants to be completely renewable. She's a massive fan of yours." Millie hesitated, biting her bottom lip. "If I'm honest," she said after a beat. "I got you and your brother confused. When I googled the company, your face didn't show up anywhere."

"Purposefully," I admitted, settling back in my seat. "I hate being in the spotlight. Give me a lab, and I'm happy. James is better at the people shit than me."

She was quiet as she watched me.

"What?" I asked as she glanced at the privacy screen that separated us from the driver.

"I saw your post. About the missed connection. It didn't click before but.... That was me, right?"

I grinned. "Yeah."

She flushed, her gaze dropping as she continued to toy with the straps of her bag. "Damn. I was hoping you hadn't seen my underwear."

Just mentioning the underwear had me wondering what she wore under her colourful skirt.

"Millie, would you come to dinner with me?"

Her head shot up, her eyebrows rising in surprise. "W-w-what? Me?"

I laughed. "Yes, you. Would you have dinner with me?"

"Why?"

Because you're intriguing. Because I'm fascinated to learn what else makes you blush. Because you're adorable, and I want nothing more than to strip away your clothing and taste what lies underneath.

"Because I want to share a meal with someone who doesn't look at me like I'm abnormal."

The words were not what I had intended. They weren't even close to what I would have admitted—even to myself.

Millie tilted her head to one side, a large chunk of her blonde locks falling across her shoulder.

"I have to admit, I do think you're extraordinary. I can't even conceptualise how you created what you've got, let alone built a business worth a billion dollars. Even a million seems outside the realm of possibility."

I remembered those days—when even a thousand dollars in my bank account seemed like a steep hill to climb.

I cleared my throat. "So, dinner?"

She flushed again, her head dropping. "Well, I guess that depends."

"On?"

She looked up at me, a teasing grin on her lips. "Can we do burgers?"

I laughed, reaching out to tuck a stray strand of hair behind her ear. "Sounds perfect."

CHAPTER 8

"**H**as he arrived yet?"

It was the weekend, a whole two days after Ash had driven me home and blown my mind by asking me out.

"No," I answered Keiko as I looked at myself in the mirror with a critical eye. "He's not meant to be here for another five minutes."

"Send me a photo. Mai and I will approve your outfit."

I snapped a selfie with me pulling a silly face and sent it to her. I heard the phone being shifted back and forth between the sisters.

As I waited for their verdict, I checked in with my body, noting the fluttering butterflies in my stomach, my increased heart rate, my slightly flushed cheeks.

Oh, Millie. You silly fool.

I knew Ash was just being nice. He was the kind of guy who surely had his pick of women —astronauts, supermodels, actresses, Nobel Peace Prize winners. There was no way he would be interested in a plump, funny but solidly average woman of dubious financial status.

Well, not so dubious anymore.

Sally had sent through the contract which contained more zeroes than Keiko and I had ever seen. Our only condition was that we landed the pitch. So much relied on us getting this right. Adding in a quick fling with the boss seemed like a terrible idea.

And yet here you are, dressed to go on a hike with a man who promises burgers, and posts missed connections that reference your underwear.

I didn't know how to feel about Ash.

Keiko interrupted any further self-deprecation efforts.

"Alright, we're in agreement. You look perfect."

I huffed out a laugh. "Your approval means everything to me, you know that."

Kei ignored my sarcastic tone. "You going to kiss him?"

I hesitated. "I'm not sure that's what this kind of date is."

"Oh, please," she scoffed. "The man couldn't take his eyes off you the whole pitch meeting. Girl, you got this. Get yourself a little slice of that nerdy man before someone else does."

I bit my lip, my nipples tingling at the thought of Ash touching me.

"What if he's just being nice?" I whispered, voicing my darkest thought.

"Babe, the man did a missed connection that generated newspaper articles. He took you home and—I note—asked you on a date as soon as he got you alone. He's into you."

My little heart skipped at her affirmation.

"Okay, I—"

A knock at the door interrupted me.

"Shit, he's here."

"Go slay him with your sweetness, Millie! Love you."

"Love you too."

I hung up, taking one last look at myself in the mirror.

"You got this, Millie. It's just a date with a guy who is into you."

"Hey," Ash greeted as I opened the door. "You look great."

If I were a cartoon my tongue would have rolled out of my mouth, my heart leaping from my chest while little love hearts flew around my head.

Oh, boy. This is totally unfair.

He wore thick worn boots, faded jeans, and a shirt under his flannel. The sleeves of it were pushed back to his elbows, revealing his biceps.

Oh, Lordy. Can I have him with whipped cream and cherries, please?

He leaned in, pressing a kiss to my cheek, my body immediately flushing at the intimate gesture.

Wowowowowowowowowowowowowowowowow!

I tried to pull myself together. I tried to stuff Ash back into the 'potential client' and 'maybe future boss' boxes in my mind. But my libido wasn't having a bar of it. That sexy bitch strode out in high heels, a see-through-teddy, and nipple tassels ready to ride this man into a lusty, fulfilling orgasm.

Well, hell.

"I have something for you." Ash twisted, pulling something from his backpack. "You can open it later."

I accepted the rectangular box, blinking at the small wonky bow in the corner.

"My niece helped me wrap it. She said it was rude to arrive on a date without a gift."

I ran my hands over the box, touched by his thoughtfulness. "Thank you."

He shifted, seemingly uncomfortable. "Shall we head off?"

I nodded. "Give me two minutes to just pop this inside and grab my bag."

I ran back in, picking up my backpack and shrugging it on as I laid the present carefully on my kitchen table. Curiosity burned within me.

I locked up, then turned to him, spreading my arms wide. "Lead on."

He pressed a hand to the small of my back, guiding me down my staircase to an electric car parked on the curb.

"No driver today?"

"I like to occasionally remind myself that I'm capable of operating a vehicle."

I grinned, my heart skipping a little when he opened my door for me.

Be still my heart, an actual gentleman.

I slipped in, admiring him as he walked around to get in the driver's side.

"So where are we going?"

He started the car, the quiet as startling now as it was when he'd last driven me home.

"I thought we'd do a hike out to Lover's Lake, then have some lunch at Pier Pressure."

"That'd be great. I've actually never been out there."

Ash cocked an eyebrow at me. "Really?"

"Yeah. I mean, I only moved to Capricorn Cove two years ago."

"Why the Cove?"

I laughed, rolling my eyes at myself. "Whimsy? No, in all seriousness, it seemed like a good idea at the time. Between the expansion of the marina a few years ago, the two cities on either side and the number of millionaires living in what is a surprisingly affordable town —it just made sense. Also, Keiko's family is from around here."

"How'd you meet?"

"We both worked in the city for the same design firm. Fresh out of college, we kind of just fell in together. We hated it. The boss was a dick, and any time a client loved our work, he took all the credit."

Ash flicked on the indicator, pulling onto a gravel road. "So, the move to being your own boss was easy?"

"Not easy. We wanted to stay in the city but couldn't swing it money-wise. When Keiko's brother, Ren, mentioned that there was a little office building down the road from the fire department that had just come on the market. When we crunched the numbers, it made sense."

"And you live above the business?"

I nodded. "I bought the building. Keiko suggested we go halves, but it just made more sense for one of us to take the financial risk. It also meant I could turn the rooms above into an actual apartment. It's not much, but it's home."

"What's next on the—"

Ash hit the brakes, twisting the car to one side of the road to avoid a deer as it leapt in front of the car, dashing across the road.

"Shit!" He twisted. "You okay?"

I nodded, forcing air into my lungs. "Damn. That was close. Good thing you weren't going faster."

"Yeah."

We both sat in silence for a moment, staring at each other.

"Would it be rude if I said I really wanna kiss you right now?" he asked, his expression shifting.

"Um, no?"

"Good."

He leaned across the console, one hand coming up to cup the back of my head, guiding me to him.

Our lips met soft at first, a slow, tender kiss.

I made a sound in my throat, my heart—

already frantic from the near-miss—pounded in my ears, need heating my blood.

Ash snapped. His mouth became greedy, his tongue licking at my lips until I opened for him—allowing him to taste me. He groaned, shifting closer.

A horn blared behind us, breaking our kiss. We stared at each other, our breathing laboured as I searched his face, reading surprised delight in his expression.

The horn blared again, breaking the spell.

We both sat back in our seats as Ash put the car in gear, resuming our journey to the lake.

I lifted a shaking hand, pressing fingertips to my overly sensitive lips.

I just kissed my new boss.

I glanced at the man in question, finding his gaze on me. A blush crept up my neck, heating my cheeks as a sinful smile stole across his lips.

"Remind me to try that again later," he said, his voice an actual caress. "I loved tasting you, Millie."

I opened my mouth to reply, but words escaped me.

Oh, Millie. What have you gotten yourself into?

CHAPTER 9

Ash

illie let out a moan, her eyes drifting shut. "Oh God," she muttered her expression pure bliss. "This is incredible."

And now I'm jealous of a beef patty.

I swallowed my own bite of burger, shoving away the jealousy.

"Pier Pressure does the best burgers this side of the lake."

Millie nodded, wiping at her lips with a napkin. "I believe it."

We'd hiked around one of the tracks, taking in the breathtaking views as I learned everything I could about this intriguing woman.

Millie was an only child of only children

but desperately wanted a big family—and was completely enamoured with the idea of mine. She loved her friends, hated pumpkin, and normally tried to go hiking once a month but loved swimming more than walking so tended to go to the beach during the warmer months. She smelled like oranges, and her laugh made me hard every single time.

She sighed, leaning back against the picnic table as we ate our meal, her gaze glued to the lake.

"What are you thinking?" I asked, selfishly wanting to know all her thoughts.

"Just that this has been a perfect date." She flushed, her head ducking. "That is—I mean—"

I reached out, capturing one of her hands and giving it a squeeze. "I have to agree."

She peeked up at me through her bangs, her expression hopeful. "Really?"

I nodded. "One hundred percent this is the best date I've ever been on."

Her smile was instantaneous and stunning. "Thank you, Ash. That means a lot."

As we finished off our burgers, the humidity began to roll in.

"There'll be a storm tonight, I think."

Millie nodded; wisps of hair that had escaped her ponytail bobbed in agreement.

I stood, collecting our rubbish. "Shall we swim?"

"I didn't bring a swimsuit."

I grinned. "Neither did I. But I know a place. We could skinny dip—"

She blushed, her face reddening at my teasing.

"—or just wear our underwear."

For a moment she hesitated, her face scarlet.

"This place, is it private?"

I nodded, separating the rubbish into organics and recyclables ready for disposal. "It's only a few minutes away."

"Alright."

We waved to the grumpy restaurant owner as we passed, exchanging an amused grin when he ignored us.

We walked in companionable silence around the lake, the trail weaving us in and out of the forest.

"How do you know about this spot?" Millie asked as I detoured off a track at a set of boulders, assisting her to scramble over the ancient stone.

"I used to come out here a lot when I was younger. My dad liked to bring us boys out to the lake to burn off steam. One summer we found this private little cove. I've only ever seen one other person here."

Sure enough, as we exited the woods, the little cove opened to us, the soft sand of the small sheltered area completely serene.

"Oh." Millie sucked in a breath. "This is delightful."

I dropped my backpack on the ground, pulling a picnic blanket free to spread across the ground. "It's not quite a towel but it will do."

I shrugged off my shirt, my flannel long abandoned, and reached for my belt. For a moment Millie hesitated, her expression unsure.

"Hey, it's just me. I can close my eyes and turn around if it helps?"

She chuckled, shaking her head. "You've already seen the goods. What's a little more, right?"

With one smooth move, she peeled her shirt off, leaving her in a simple black bra.

I nearly swallowed my tongue at the wealth of skin she revealed, her curves on display as she kicked off her shoes, pushing her jeans down her legs and stepping free.

She's wearing cookie underwear.

Across the front were the words *'made for*

each other' with a cookie and a glass of milk holding hands.

Why does her underwear turn me on so much?

She grinned pointing at her crotch. "I have a thing for cute prints."

There was something in my throat as I answered hoarsely, "I can tell."

Her gaze dropped to my hands resting on my belt. "You gonna strip too? Or was this a ploy to see my underwear?"

I grinned, beginning to move. "If I said yes, what would you do?"

She flushed but maintained eye contact. "Probably try and push you into the lake."

I chuckled, discarding my jeans on the blanket. "Come on, let's cool off."

We stepped in, both of us sighing as the calm water cooled our heated skin.

Millie swam beside me, her head tilting back as she sank down into the water, her eyelids drifting shut.

"Heaven," she murmured.

Yeah, you are.

My skin may have cooled but my blood felt like fire. A drop of water ran down her neck, hovering on the curve of one breast. The desire to lick it from her skin nearly overwhelmed me.

"Thank you, Ash."

I met her gaze, raising an eyebrow in question. "For?"

She lifted a hand, giving one lazy gesture to encompass the area. "This. It's given me an insight into who you are." Her head tilted, her lips curving into a teasing smile. "You're not all work, which is what I was expecting."

I shifted, coming to float beside her. "Would it kill the mood if you know I'll have to log on tonight and make up some time?"

She laughed, shaking her head. "I'll be doing the same. Such is the life of the boss, right?"

"Do you ever wish you weren't?"

Millie considered my question, her hands lazily gliding through the water. "Sometimes. Mostly when we have a bad month and I have to work out how to keep the lights on. Or when we're dealing with a particularly difficult client. It's hard, you know?"

I nodded. "Two years ago, we sold off an arm of the business—we needed the capital, and the buying company had more expertise in manufacturing that kind of product. It was a win-win all round." I shook my head. "I still have nightmares about the faces of my employees when we announced it."

Millie reached out, her fingers grazing my skin. "Is that why you work so hard?"

"Probably. I have a responsibility to my employees. To their families."

"But what about to yourself?"

I shrugged, a spike of emotion digging into my chest. "If I'm honest, for a long time work was enough."

"Now?" she asked.

"Now," I paused, unsure of how she might take this. "Now, I find myself distracted by memories of burgers and zippers that won't open."

Her breath caught, her eyes widening.

"Now." I reached out, cupping her cheek. "Now, I find myself thinking of how to draw the curve of a cheek rather than how to get an intake valve to work."

I leaned in, my lips hovering a breath away from hers. "Let me kiss you, Millie. Let me taste you."

She nodded, the movement brushing our lips together. "Yes."

I pulled her to me, her legs automatically wrapping around me under the water, her body moulding to mine.

Under the hot summer sun, in the cool of the lake, I kissed the woman who I knew I'd one day marry.

Marry?

I'd known her less than a combined twenty-four hours and yet I knew. I knew she was my one.

Against her lips, as I tasted her sweetness, I grinned.

After a long kiss, I drew back, determined to woo this woman and not rush her.

"Millie?"

"Mm?"

"Go out with me again. Tonight. Tomorrow night. Any day. You pick."

I want all your nights and days.

She blinked up at me, her eyes wide. "You want—really?"

"Definitely."

Her smile set my body on fire. "Okay."

To seal our future date—and because I couldn't help myself—I kissed her again.

CHAPTER 10

Millie

"And finally, we'd like to thank Thorn and Kei Designs for organising this launch. From the start, their pitch aligned with our values—to always give back. Their idea to partner with *Safe Sip* is the reason we're all here tonight." Ash held up his glass, tipping it towards Keiko and me. "Thank you."

The crowd applauded as the master of ceremonies concluded the official speeches, a swarm of people surging to surround Ash as he stepped off the stage.

We'd organised the water filter launch to be held at Lover's Lake Lodge—the building a triumph of old glass and wood that showcased the beautiful water views in the early twilight.

The lodge had been here for over a century, with extensions and renovations keeping it pristine and relevant in the modern age.

Apart from the views, we'd also sold Ash and James on Lover's Lake Lodge because the owners believed in being carbon neutral. They'd invested significant capital to become an eco-lodge, the first in Capricorn Cove.

Sally hadn't been thrilled—complaining that it was a waste to hold the launch in some pokey little corner of a pokey little town when the city was right there.

I spotted her in the far corner, a pissed-off expression on her face as she stared at Ash.

"He's driving me crazy," I admitted to Keiko as we watched Ash shake hands and smile at his adoring fans. "I just want to rip his clothes off and ride him into next week."

I'd been officially dating Ash for three weeks, and each moment had me falling a little bit more in love with the guy.

Not to mention becoming even hornier.

I wanted him—desperately. But the guy kept everything above the belt and over clothes. It was driving me bonkers.

Keiko reached for another shrimp, juggling it with the champagne in her hand. "Then make your move. The man can't keep his hands off you."

And yet he keeps his clothes on.

I watched Ash interact with the head of the clean water charity, his expression serious as he listened to the woman explain something.

"He really is the most attractive of men," I sighed, leaning against Keiko.

She bumped my hip. "And you are the most attractive of women. Go on, Millie. Ask him to dance."

I shook my head. "It'll attract too much attention. You know Ash hates it when he's in the spotlight."

Keiko rolled her eyes. "Then I will if you—"

"Ladies," James, Ash's brother interrupted us. "May I steal Millie away? My brother is dying to dance with her but won't ask while he's still got big wigs to satisfy." He sent me a wink. "I—on the other hand—have zero compulsions and am more than willing to ensure he has fun tonight."

"By making his girlfriend dance with you?" Keiko asked, cocking one eyebrow.

"By making him jealous." He held out a big hand, wiggling his blunt fingers at me. "Come on, live a little."

Keiko gave me a little push, sending me tripping into James' arms. "Go! Dance! I shall hold down this delicious buffet."

I laughed, allowing James to escort me onto the dance floor.

"You know," I said as he spun me away and then back into his arms. "I have to admit to being stunned that you're so light on your feet."

"Boxing," he said with a grin, leading me across the dance floor. "My coach insisted on dance lessons. Said it made you a better boxer."

Over his shoulder, I saw his executive assistant talking with her fiancé, neither looked happy.

"Is Hazel okay?"

James turned us so he could watch the heated exchange, his face hardening.

"No. She's engaged to an absolute jackass of a—" James cut himself off, shaking his head. "Sorry. I shouldn't have said that."

"It's okay. You love her. I get that."

His expression froze, his feet tripping for a moment before he quickly righted himself.

"Shit. Is it that obvious?"

I blinked at his tone. "Well, no. I meant as in a friendship kind of love. James.... Are you *in* love with her?"

He closed his eyes, huffing out a laugh. "Fuck."

My heart ached at the pain in his voice.

"Have you told her?"

He shook his head. "She's been with the

jackass for years. What was I meant to do? Declare my undying love at her engagement party?"

I squeezed his hand. "I'm sorry."

"Yeah, me too."

We danced around the floor, James turning me this way and that—his gaze drifting repeatedly towards his pretty assistant.

"Do me a favour?" he asked as the song began to wrap up.

"Anything."

He looked over my shoulder, his gaze narrowing. "If you love someone, don't wait to tell them. You don't know what tomorrow might bring."

With that, he pasted on a smile that came nowhere close to his eyes and stepped back, turning me slightly. Ash approached, his gaze fixed on me.

"Hey bro, about time you joined us." James held out my hand to Ash as the band struck up another song. "Have fun you two."

The CFO disappeared into the crowd, leaving Ash and me on the dance floor.

We considered each other for a moment, our gazes heated as his thumb dragged slowly along the inside of my wrist.

"You look beautiful."

I dropped my gaze, pleasure blooming in my belly. "Thank you."

His gaze dropped to my outfit. "You're wearing the dress."

I pressed a hand to the dress that had brought us together. "Mm. Though the zipper is a little faulty." A hot blush heated my cheeks as I propositioned him. "Do you know anyone who might be able to help get me out of it?"

He swore, drawing the gazes of the couples around us.

In one smooth move, he stepped in, one hand entwined with mine, his other pressing into the small of my back.

"You'll be the death of me," he whispered against my temple as we began to sway together. "I'm trying not to rush you, Millie.

I hesitated. "What if I want to be rushed?"

Ash's hands flinched. "What are you saying?"

I licked my lips, calling on all my courage to look up into his glorious green eyes. "Ash, what do you want from me?"

His expression changed, his eyes flashing. "Everything."

Desire spiked. "Then take me to bed. Make love to me."

He stopped moving. Around us, the world

continued to revolve as people shifted across the dance floor, lost in the music.

"Now?" he asked, his voice hoarse.

"Have you finished with all the formalities?" I asked, ignoring the curious glances we were drawing.

"Yes."

"Then yes."

He moved, leading me off the dance floor with a hand on my back. People moved out of our way, parting for their prince among men.

I glanced at the buffet, finding Keiko grinning as she watched us. She caught my gaze, lifting her glass in a silent salute.

My blush deepened, my body tingling as anticipation began to bubble in my belly.

I'm going to make love to Ash.

I tipped my head back, glancing up at the gorgeous man beside me. His expression was tight, his body wired as he navigated the ballroom.

I can't wait.

CHAPTER 11

Ash

Fuck. I can't wait to taste her.

Need drove me hard. Desire warring with reason as I tried to work out where to take Millie.

Home? The pier? A spare closet?

A small door off to one side of the hall gave me pause. With a backward glance, I opened it, pulling Millie into an abandoned cloakroom.

"Ash! What are you—"

I cut her off with a kiss, backing her up until I could press her against a wall. Her curves moulded against my body, spiking my need for her.

Fuck.

I wanted my mouth on her pussy. I wanted to taste her cream.

I reached down, fisting the bottom of her skirt and pulling it up her legs. She moaned under me, deepening our kiss.

That's it, sweetness. Let me taste.

As our mouths fucked, I tangled one hand in the soft strands of her hair holding her still as my other hand slipped under the skirt of her dress, grazing up her inner thighs.

I drew back, satisfaction rolling through me at the sight of her swollen lips.

"You okay?" I asked, voice rough as my hand moved to cup her, pleased at the damp material under my palm.

"Oh!" Millie's head dropped back against the wall, her body arching into mine. "Y-yes."

I grinned, trying to control the raging inferno of need inside me.

"Are you going to...." Her hips moved, completing her unfinished question.

"Oh, yeah."

I dropped to my knees, shimmying her dress up until I could part her legs, revealing her sexy body to my gaze.

"Oh, Millie."

She looked down, her hand tangling in my hair. "Do you like it?"

I grinned, hooking fingers into the lace of

her panties, pulling them down her body. "They're fucking sexy, sweetness. But I'll always prefer the burger print."

I lowered my head, my mouth closing over her. Immediately she let out a whimper, her head dropped back to the wall, her hands reaching out in desperation as she gripped me.

"Ash!"

I didn't hold back. Desire rode me hard as I licked my woman. Millie's panting whimpers turned into moans, her hips moving in time with my mouth as I teased and taunted, playing her body.

"Ash," Millie panted, her fingers digging into my scalp. "I'm gonna... I'm...."

I stared up at her hungrily, desperate to watch her fall apart. "Come, sweetness. Come on my tongue." I dipped my head, finding her clit, teasing her until she broke.

"Ash!"

Millie arched off the wall, her hips bucking as she came. I steadied her with my hands, holding her up when she would have slid to the floor. I stood, pulling her into me, desperate to lift her up and fill her with my cock—but determined to ensure this would be the best night of her life.

She's mine. She's my future. This is the start of everything.

"Ash...." She looked up at me, her eyes bright. "I-I-I...."

I grinned, pressing my forehead against hers. "I know."

Her hands dropped to my suit pants, my cock tenting the material.

"Millie, no, wait—"

"No. I need you. Please."

Fuck. I can't deny you anything.

In a fumble of fingers, we shoved my pants down, freeing my cock. I bit out a curse as Millie's hand wrapped around my dick.

"Like this?" she asked with a teasing grin as she jerked me.

"Fuck yes," I groaned.

I need to taste her.

With rough hands, I jerked the bodice of Millie's dress down, shoving the cups of her bra up, revealing her perfect breasts to my hungry gaze.

"Fucking beautiful. You're fucking magnificent, Millie. Perfect."

She flushed, her body arching as my lips enclosed one nipple, tasting her skin.

Mine.

"Ash. Ash, condom?'

Fuck.

I sucked on her breast, grazing teeth over

her heated skin then released her with a pop, reaching down to pull my wallet free.

Shit, how long has it been in here? Condoms expire. Shit. It's been like, what? Six years since I put this in here? When did Dad give me the birds and bees talk? How long do—

My thoughts cut off when Millie plucked it from my hands, dropping to her knees before me.

"Millie, what are you—Fuck!"

Her lips closed around my cock, her body shifting forward as she sucked me deep into her throat.

"I love you," I bit out, my eyes rolling back in my head. "You're the only one for me, Millie. Just you, sweetness. Just—"

She pulled free, rolling the condom down my cock, her smile bright in the dim light.

"Maybe wait till after we've consummated to decide if you want to propose," she whispered, sending me a wink.

Oh, baby. Don't you know I'd marry you tonight if I could?

I helped her stand, my hands cupping her bottom lifting her up, helping to position her against the wall, her legs wrapping tight around my waist. "Ready?"

She nodded, her body tensing for my intrusion.

"Guide me in, sweetness."

With wide eyes, Millie reached down, lining me up. I worked myself inside her, both of us groaning as I breached her entrance.

"Fuck, Millie." I dropped a hot kiss to her mouth, nearly cross-eyed as her body began to welcome me. "Perfect for me. Fucking perfect."

"Gonna move," I told her, need tingling at the small of my back. "Ready?"

She nodded, her arms and legs tightening around me as her pussy melted, welcoming my length.

I pulled back, thrusting in with violent intention.

"Ash!" Her body arching into mine.

"Right here," I grunted, gritting my teeth, determined to make this perfect for my woman. "Open for me, sweetness. Let me fill your pretty little pussy."

I rode her hard, fucking into her with ruthless brutality, determined to mark her, to brand her as mine.

"Fuck," I groaned as I felt her orgasm rip through her, her pussy milking my cock in the tightest, most pleasurable experience known to man. "Millie!"

I came, spilling inside her, unable to see straight.

Spent, I collapsed against the wall, leaning

her back against it, holding us both up for a long moment, our skin cooling.

"Ash?"

"Mm?" I murmured, pressing kisses against the sensitive skin at her neck.

"At least we didn't need to struggle with a zipper."

For a moment I had no idea what she was talking about, then it registered—the fucking dress.

I laughed as I pressed a kiss to her smiling lips.

"Cheeky minx." I squeezed her tight then let her slip down my body, enjoying the feel of her against me. "Let's head to your place. I want to try that again—but with a bed this time."

CHAPTER 12

Millie

"And then?" Keiko asked, her eyes wide as she stared at me, sucking down a green juice.

"And then he took me home, ripped my dress off me, and we made love until the early morning." I sighed, my heart giving a happy little skip at the memory. "He had to leave early for a work meeting but made me coffee and toast and promised to call after lunch."

Keiko groaned, laying a hand over her eyes dramatically. "Be still my heart. Does he have a brother?"

"Actually, a few—but one is still in high school."

She grinned, flicking her hair. "I'm ready to

be a cougar—just give me some leopard print pants and a tube top."

I laughed, pushing her chair away with my foot. "Don't lie—I know you've been eyeing off one of the bodyguards for that singer who lives in town."

She lifted an eyebrow. "What makes you say that?"

"Uh." I raised a finger to my chin pretending to think. "Let's see. You hate green juice but there you are every morning at the juice store ordering one at the precise time he also happens to be there."

She rolled her eyes, sucking another sip down with a grimace. "A coincidence. I'm trying to be healthier."

"You started going to the gym when—and I quote—you would rather be tarred and feathered than wear spandex."

She shrugged. "I purchased bamboo and nylon."

"And—and this is the kicker—you drool every time he walks by."

Kei picked up a pen, throwing it at my head. "Shut your pie hole!"

"You shut your—"

My cell rang, interrupting our shenanigans.

"It's Sally." I exchanged a confused look with Keiko.

"Did we miss a meeting?"

I shook my head, reaching for the phone. "Nope, we're not due for a check-in until Thursday." I swiped my thumb across the screen and hit loudspeaker. "Hello?"

"Ms. Hawthorn? This is Sally Turner."

"Hi Sally, how can I help you today?"

"I'm calling about last night's launch."

I grinned, shooting Keiko a wink. "Didn't it go wonderfully? I was so pleased to—"

"Your services are no longer required."

I stuttered to a halt. "I'm sorry?"

"In light of the news article published today, your contract with us has been terminated. We will, of course, pay you for the work you completed in relation to the launch but due to inappropriate behaviour, our contract is now null and void."

"I'm sorry, can you please—"

"The money will be transferred into your bank account shortly. I've requested that all access to the building be removed. Goodbye, Ms. Hawthorn."

"Sally, wait! I—"

The phone made a sad sound before ending.

I stared at it for a beat then looked up, my eyes wide as I met Keiko's shocked gaze.

"Did that just—"

"What the fuck was—"

Kei pulled her phone from her pocket, fingers flying across the screen.

"Oh shit."

"What?" I leaned over, trying to see her screen. "Did something go wrong?"

"Um... do you want the good news or the bad news?"

"There's worse news than us getting fired?" I yelped.

Kei glanced over at me; her phone pressed to her chest. "Bad or good, Millie?"

I tried to breathe, feeling as if I were wearing a vice around my chest.

"Bad. Hit me."

She turned the phone my way, the image dark but clearly capturing Ash in a dishevelled state as he did the walk of shame from my apartment. The news had broken an hour ago.

"Oh God," I breathed, closing my eyes and dropping my face into my hands. "He's gonna hate this." I opened one eye, peeking at Kei through my fingers. "What's the good news?"

She pointed out our sign in the background of the image. "Free international advertising?"

I groaned, sinking into my seat. "I need to call Ash."

"Yeah, you do. That woman was a bitch

and completely out of line. You might be screwing a client—"

I moaned again.

"—but it's consensual. Two hot-as-fuck humans just getting their kit on. Nothing to be ashamed of. You were also employed *before* he knew who you were."

I reached for my phone, my heart in my throat. "Let me call him. I'm sure we can work it out."

I hit his number, waiting for it to ring.

"We're sorry, you have reached a number that has been disconnected or is no longer in service."

I blinked, staring at my phone.

"Did you put it in wrong?"

"I... maybe?"

I typed the number out, double-checking it before hitting call again.

"We're sorry, you have reached a number that has been disconnected or is no longer in service."

I slowly raised my head, shock turning the world black and white as my heart died a little.

"Kei... I think he's dumped me."

"Babe, you can't know that. It could just be a—"

I shook my head slowly, bile burning up the back of my throat.

"I think this is his way of ghosting me."

"Oh, Millie."

A tear slipped down my cheek as Keiko leaned forward, wrapping me in a tight hug.

"I never should have believed a billionaire could fall in love with me."

Keiko gave me a little shake. "He should be so lucky!" She pressed a kiss to my hair. "Ice cream?"

I shook my head, my stomach clenching as the reality of what had happened hit me. "We're back to square one. Without that money coming in we're only going to be able to float for another month or two at best."

She squeezed me tight. "We'll work it out. We always do."

I took some solace in that, knowing she was right. We'd made it this far on a whim and prayer. Our business would survive.

My heart meanwhile? Only time would tell.

CHAPTER 13

Ash

A commotion interrupted my chain of thought.

I looked up from the intake I'd been perfecting to see Dylan arguing with Sally. With a frown, I shoved up from my desk, heading out to reception.

"Problem?" I asked, leaning against my door.

"Mr. Dogg." Sally turned to me, her expression pinched. "We need to talk. Immediately."

"And I," Dyl said, looking extremely put out. "Have already told you he's not to be disturbed."

Sally slapped a printed piece of paper

down on Dylan's desk, pointing at it. "Read it and tell me this isn't an emergency."

I walked across, picking up the paper to scan the contents.

Who is Ash Dogg's hook-up?

The article was a fluff piece from a known gossip news outlet.

"As you can see, the article is damning. I've taken the liberty of firing the offending contractor, and have organised for a new number and email to be provided to you immediately." Sally crossed her arms, a satisfied smile painting her face. "The press release will make it clear that you have had only minimal contact with Ms. Hawthorn, and that any implied intimacy is an inaccurate observation."

I stared at this woman before me, stunned at her self-entitled air.

"You did what?"

"I fired Thorn and Kei Designs this morning."

For a moment my world shifted, my body jerking in denial.

Millie.

"Sally?" I asked, barely able to control the rage in my voice.

"Yes?"

"You're fired."

She stared at me, her hands dropping. "What?"

"Fired." I turned to Dylan. "Call security. I want Ms. Turner removed from the premises immediately."

Dyl nodded, their thoughts hidden behind a mask of cool indifference. "Will do."

"What do you think you're doing? You can't fire me! I just saved—"

"Stop."

I turned back around, pegging her with a glare. Rage boiled my blood. I wanted to rip something apart.

I'd never hit a woman, never even contemplated it. But I was having definite visions of destroying whatever was left of this woman's career.

Calm down. This isn't about her; this is about Millie.

"Ash, you can't be serious. This is—"

I stepped forward, drawing up to my full height.

"This," I said, my tone low and deadly. "Is my company. *Mine.*" I punctuated my point with a finger to my chest. "*I* am the CEO. *I* am the founder. And *I* am a man in love with a woman. With Millie Hawthorn to be exact. That picture, Ms. Turner, is *exactly* what it looks like. And I don't regret a goddamned fucking minute of it. You've put at risk my future. You overstepped. You fucked up. And I don't tolerate fuck ups."

I looked to Dyl. "Clear my calendar. I'm taking a leave of absence."

Dyl's mask shattered, happiness dancing in their eyes. "You're going to Millie, aren't you?"

"You bet your fucking ass I am."

I brushed passed Sally, heading for the elevator, rage still surging through my veins as I stabbed at the button.

"Ash, I—"

I glared at the protesting woman.

"Goodbye, Sally. And, if I were you, I'd find a job in another city. Fuck, in another country. No one I know is gonna hire you if I have anything to say about it—I guarantee it."

With that, the doors closed and I refocused on what was important.

Getting to Millie.

CHAPTER 14

Millie

The account books sat in front of me, my eyes feeling like sandpaper as I stared at the numbers attempting to work out how to stretch our income.

Maybe if we—

"Oh, fuck no!" Keiko called from the reception area. "Absolutely fucking not! Get out!"

"Keiko, I—"

My heart clenched at Ash's familiar voice.

"No!" Kei yelled; her tone furious. "You're a fucking traitor. You hurt the most wonderful woman I know! Do you have any idea how much she cried? Dude, you're a fucking—"

"Idiot! I know! I should have fired Sally five

minutes after she was hired. Instead, it took this to prompt me."

Wait. What?

"Wait," Keiko echoed my thoughts. "What?"

"Please Kei, I need to see her."

I sat frozen at my desk, straining to hear their discussion now whispered. Just as I was about to crack, Ash appeared in my doorway, Keiko hovering behind him.

"Millie."

I swallowed, my stomach feeling as if I'd been punched as he stared at me.

I stood slowly, my emotions as brittle as glass.

This is it. This is him breaking up with you. Officially.

I lifted my chin, stiffening my spine. "Go ahead," I invited, proud that my voice didn't waver. "I can take it."

"I love you."

His words didn't register—they were so foreign, so removed, so opposite to what I'd expected that I couldn't process them.

"What?"

He moved into my office, coming around my desk to drop to his knees in front of me. From the corner of my eye I saw a smiling Keiko close the door, shutting us in.

"I love you, Millie. I know it's too soon. I know it's irrational. I know this is the worst possible moment after the clusterfuck that was Sally. But it's true. I've been falling in love with you since I saw your burger underwear."

He caught my hand, holding it tight as I stared down at him, mute with shock.

"When Sally told me what she did, I dropped everything to be here. You're all that matters. Losing you, the thought of it—" He broke off, shaking his head. "It rips me a-fucking-part."

He pulled an envelope from his pocket, handing it to me. "Sally wanted to publish a media release explaining that we were nothing to each other. I decided to rewrite it to describe what I hope we could be."

As he watched I opened the envelope, pulling a piece of paper free. With shaking hands, I unfolded the sheet, reading the handwritten release.

Billionaire marries burger babe

Ash Dogg, Founder and CEO of Dogg Wood Industries, is proud to announce his marriage to Millie Hawthorn, Founder, and CEO of

Thorn and Kei Designs. The two were married in a private ceremony in the small town of Capricorn Cove following a whirlwind romance.

"When I look at Millie, I see my future. She's all I've ever wanted. She's all I'll ever want. She's the love of my life."

Mr. Dogg and Ms. Hawthorn will honeymoon before returning to the Cove to live happily ever after.

I looked up, a strange fluttering feeling taking residence in my chest.

"I love you, Millie." From his pocket he withdrew a ring, holding it out to me. "I'm sorry. I'm so *fucking* sorry you have no idea. But know this. If you say yes, if you take me right now, then I want to do it right. I want you to marry me. I want to journey through this life with you. I want to have a family, have a future, have a life that involves you."

I stared into his eyes, searching for any sign he might have doubts. Looking for any hesitancy.

There was none to be found.

I cleared my throat. "I have conditions."

He froze, the ring still held out to me. "Anything."

"One weekend a month we have a strict no-work policy."

His lips twitched, relief softening his face. "Agreed."

"And no work after nine unless it's a call internationally. And then you have to go into work later the next morning."

His smile grew. "Absolutely."

"And we take two vacations a year."

"Counter—four."

I raised an eyebrow. "Four?"

"Yeah. One each season."

I smiled, my heart lifting. "Alright. Four. And here's my final condition."

His face sobered, his gaze intense as I dropped to my knees, reaching out to cup his hand.

"You have to love me forever. Though all the seasons of life. When I'm flustered in a ballroom or getting stuck in prison dresses. When we're happy in bed, or struggling with exhaustion. You have to, Ash. Every single day."

"I swear." His voice was guttural, his expression fierce. "Every single day."

"Then yes, I'll marry you."

He twisted our hands, moving so he was holding mine, sliding the ring on my finger.

"Oh," I whispered, staring at the giant rock. "It's too much."

Even Millionaire Millie was impressed.

"It's perfect for you." He leaned in, pressing a kiss to my finger. "I love you, Millie."

I melted, sighing as he wrapped me in his arms. "And I love you, Ash."

"Forever?"

"And ever, and ever," I promised and sealed it with a kiss.

CHAPTER 15

"Is your dog having a spa day?"

Dylan glanced over their shoulder, flicking me a grin. "Yes."

The dog in question was one of those creepy-looking hairless things that in some weird way was also cute.

Smothered in cream, Dylan appeared to be painting the pup's nails a bright pink shade.

"I'd ask for more information but—to be honest—I really don't want to know."

Dyl lifted one shoulder in a half-shrug. "All you need to know is that Ms. Pepper loves her pamper time."

Ms. Pepper was Dylan's newest rescue.

I held up my hands in surrender. "Again, don't want to know."

I moved to walk into my office but was stopped by Dylan.

"Boss, I'd check out the conference room if I were you." They lifted one hand, pointing down the hall with the tip of their nail polish brush. "You have a meeting."

I raised an eyebrow. "I do?"

"Mmhmm." They continued to paint Ms. Pepper's nails as the dog lay snoozing on a heated towel.

I blew out a breath. "You know, Dyl. One day I might feel as if we're a professional operation."

"Today," they said, gently applying the polish. "Is not that day."

I laughed, twisting on my heel. "Get back to work."

"I am working!"

I walked down the hall, wracking my brain to remember which meeting I was about to walk into.

The engine issue is sorted, and we're in testing. I met the financial team yesterday. The launch team are in full-steam-ahead mode and scheduled to meet tomorrow. Our new PR isn't due to start until Monday. Who the hell am I meeting with?

I shoved the door of the conference room open, stumbling to a halt in the entry, my gaze jumping around the room.

"What on—"

"Surprise!"

Millie threw her arms out, a giant smile on her face as my family, Keiko, and a small group of employees crowded around her, all of them laughing and smiling at my stunned expression. "Welcome to your logo launch."

I stared at the giant plant on the conference table, utterly speechless.

It's perfect.

A topiary tree's limbs were fashioned into the shape of a light bulb. Carved into a piece of old wood mounted on the wall were the words, *Green ideas grow here.*

"Do you like it?" Millie asked, dancing from foot to foot as my family watched on.

"It's perfect."

"Oh, thank the gods." She stepped into my open arms, wrapping me in a tight hug. "I was so scared you'd hate it."

"It's...." I trailed off, searching the room to find James. He hovered near the back, his dark eyes meeting mine. He grinned, jerking his thumb at the slogan behind him.

"It fits, right?"

I nodded, forever thankful that I'd been

able to share this journey with my best friend and brother.

"Well," Jay stepped forward, clapping me on the back. "You're ready to conquer the world now."

I cocked an eyebrow at him. "Because of a logo?"

He chuckled. "No, idiot. Because you found your other half."

The woman in my arms flushed furiously. "Jay!"

"What?" He shrugged innocently. "Just saying." He leaned in, pressing a quick kiss to her cheek. "Welcome to the family, Millie."

As my brother strolled away, I looked down, my heart full of love for this magnificent woman.

"He's the Wood part of Dogg Wood Industries, right?" Millie asked, watching Jay.

I nodded. "Jay fronted us the seed money and bought our first warehouse when we outgrew the garage. He's a silent partner. Owns ten percent of the company."

"So, he's a billionaire as well?"

I nodded.

Millie looked pointedly at Jay's feet. "Then why is he wearing crocs?"

I laughed. "Because he knows it'll piss his

wife off, they'll fight, then he'll get make-up sex later."

Millie snuggled back into me. "I'll note that for our future."

Possessive joy burned through me at her words.

I leaned down, cupping her face, capturing her gaze and holding it.

"I love you, Millie."

She grinned, standing on tiptoe to press an enthusiastic kiss to my lips. "I love you too. Now let's eat some cake."

I caught her hand, pulling her into me.

"I have a better idea."

We snuck out of the conference room, leaving my family and employees celebrating the logo.

Dylan looked up from where they were massaging the moisturiser into Ms. Pepper.

"Oh, I know that look." Dyl rolled their eyes. "Go, I shall be your nookie gatekeeper yet again."

I grinned, shooting them a grin. "Have I told you lately that I love you?"

"Yes—but you also told me you'd give me a raise."

"And a triple Christmas bonus," I agreed, shoving open my office door as Millie followed, giggling and blushing behind me.

"It better be!"

I knocked the door closed with my hip, pressing Millie back against it as the blinds began to lower, closing us in.

"Need you, sweetness."

She sighed, leaning into me. "Need you too."

I loved the breathy note in her voice, the way her pupils dilated as I stroked my thumb over her bottom lip.

"We really should stop doing this," she said, her blush deepening. "It's not fair to poor Dylan."

"They'll get over it," I promised, nuzzling her neck. "I mean, I allow them to bring Ms. Pepper to the office every day. They owe me."

She huffed out a moaning laugh as I bit down gently on the curve of her neck. "Ash...."

I loved how she said my name as I warmed her blood. Loved how her body turned soft and pliant under my hands. Loved how she stretched around my cock as I came inside her.

I captured her mouth, tasting mint and heat, claiming Millie as my own.

"Missed you," I whispered between kisses.

"It's been two hours."

"Far too long."

Her hands slid down my front to fumble at

my belt, my cock straining against my zipper as she fought to free me.

I groaned as her hands fisted my length, my eyes closing at the pleasure.

"Oh, sweetness. What would I do without you?"

"Likely finish some work," the saucy minx said with a laugh.

"Turn around."

She pivoted immediately, bracing her hands against the solid door of my office. I gently brushed hair away from her neck, then ran my hands slowly down her back and sides, ensuring I hit every one of her sensitive spots.

"Hurry," she whispered, shivering under my palms. "We won't have long with your family in the building."

My hands fisted the material of her skirt, lifting the material until I could reveal her to me.

"Oh, sweetness. You've been a *very* naughty girl."

My gaze swept across the generous curve of her naked ass.

She wiggled a little, sending me a blushing look over her shoulder. "Ash, hurry!"

With a groan, I fisted my cock, leaning in to run the head up her slit, coating myself in her wet heat.

"Ready?" I asked, pressing a kiss into her shoulder.

"Hurry!"

I surged forward, both of us gasping at my intrusion. Her sweet pussy clutched me like a vice, her body wet and welcoming as I began to lazily pump in and out, revelling in the little begging whimpers that escaped from Millie.

"More," she whispered, her hips shifting under my hands. "More."

I didn't change pace, working to build her need up, forcing her desire higher. Then as she looked back, her eyes bright and desperate—I unleashed, holding her hips steady as I thrust into her with violent delight, both of us gasping as we drove each other wild.

"Ash, I'm gonna—" Millie gasped, her voice breaking as her body arched, her pussy milking my cock.

"Millie!" I thrust once, twice, then spilled into her, holding my woman tight as we both came.

Desire still fizzled through my blood as I returned to myself, a delicious lethargy settling in my bones.

Mine. She's mine.

"Ash?"

"Mm?"

She twisted a little to smile up at me. "Your

family is totally gonna know we did this, aren't they?"

I leaned in to kiss her lips. "Oh, yeah." I laughed at her disgruntled expression laughing.

She blew out a sigh as I pressed my forehead against hers.

"Well, I guess we'll just have to do the walk of shame."

"Or we could stay here and make love again?" I countered.

She laughed, kissing me again. "You wish, buddy."

"Yeah, I do."

Millie shook her head, pulling back. "Come on, let's go."

With regret I allowed her to slip from my arms, watching as she straightened her skirt, pulling underwear from her pocket to slide up her legs. I reached out, catching her hand before she stepped into them.

"Burgers?" I asked, grinning at the familiar material.

"They're your favourite, right?"

I laughed, pulling her into me and kissing the laughter on her lips.

"Always."

EPILOGUE ONE

Ash

One year later

I opened one eye, grinning as Millie's fingers brushed across my cheekbones, trailing down my neck, across my chest, and down, down, down in slow, deliberate strokes.

My cock hardened, aching as she dragged her nails across my nipples, her rings flashing in the early morning light. On our bedroom wall behind her hung the picture I'd drawn of her after that first meeting—the same picture I'd given her on our first date.

"Good morning, wife."

She grinned, pressing a kiss to my nipple. "Good morning, husband."

I rolled, moving onto my side to watch her. "Is there something I can help you with, Ms. Hawthorn?"

She giggled, leaning in to press a kiss to my neck. "Maybe...."

"Only maybe?" I asked, stroking a hand lazily down her side.

She shivered under my palm, my cock responding in kind.

"Are you seducing me, Ms. Hawthorn?"

Her breath caught, her eyes flashing with desire. "Oh, yes."

I rolled to my back, spreading my arms out wide. "Then have at it, sweetness."

She climbed over me, her generous curves moulding into me as our lips met, my tongue pressing forward until I tasted her sweetness.

Millie reached up, cupping my face, the scent of her perfuming her fingers.

"Did you touch yourself?" I asked, turning my face to nip at her fingers.

She nodded; her eyes dark with desire.

"Fuck." I sat up, heaving her across my lap, positioning her until her beautiful breasts were at mouth level.

"What were you thinking of?" I asked, watching as her nipples peaked, my mouth watering for a taste. "What were you imagining, sweetness?"

"You. And that time in Lake Como with the boat, when we—"

I swore, leaning forward to capture one nipple in my mouth.

"Ash!"

I raised a hand, one thumb gently teasing her other breast. She arched under me, a low moan escaping her. I made a sound in the back of my throat, delighted at her responsiveness.

It took all my willpower to pull away, turning my head to lave her right breast, mentally apologising for my neglect.

I'm sorry, baby. I'll make it up to you.

"Ash," Millie groaned, arching against my mouth. "I want your cock."

Yeah, you do.

I dropped one hand to press my fingers against her core. With gentle touches, I began to build her up, circling her clit then dancing away, pressing and soothing, building and easing until my hand was coated in the heat of her want.

Millie arched backward, her hips undulating at my touch.

One little orgasm then you can ride me.

I built her up again—touching her until she

shattered, coming hard and yet sweetly, her every reaction perfect.

My Millie.

I pulled away, murmuring gentle words as I comforted her, loving the way her body quaked with aftershocks.

My cock throbbed, pressing urgently against her pussy, precum leaking freely.

I need to be in her.

I couldn't stop myself. I guided my cock to her entrance, pressing against her hot centre, both of us moaning as I drew the crown of my cock through her slick wet heat, covering myself in her desire.

"Ash...."

Her breathy little begging drove me wild, shattering my control.

I thrust into her, fucking up, both of us groaning as I filled her tight snatch.

Mine.

Her muscles clamped around my dick, gripping me tighter than a vice. Pleasure rioted through my body, every part of me attuned to her.

Don't come. Don't come. Fuck, dude. Don't come!

"Ride me."

Millie went crazy at my order, her body undulating as she fucked herself onto my cock, my hands holding her steady as she threw herself into the moment.

Fucking magnificent.

The need to come was near impossible to fight.

Millie first. Millie always comes first.

I dropped one hand, finding her clit, pressing in. Above me, her body shaking, she shattered, groaning as her hips bucked wildly, her body milking every last drop of cum from my cock.

Fuck!

I fell backward, bringing her down with me, our mouths meeting in a hungry kiss.

"Perfect. You're fucking perfect, sweetness."

She chuckled, tucking herself into me. "You're not too bad yourself."

"Millie?"

"Mm?"

I pressed a kiss to her forehead. "I think we got it that time."

She huffed out a laugh. "That's what you said last time."

"No really, I think that was the one."

She patted me on the shoulder, laughter in her voice. "We'll see in a few weeks. And if not, then we'll just have to keep practising."

I rolled her, hovering above my woman, my world held in my arms.

"Just saying, even if you're pregnant, we're gonna keep practising." I nuzzled at her neck, enjoying her familiar orange smell. "After all, one doesn't become a master by giving up."

She giggled, shoving at my head. "I love you."

"Love you too, sweetness. Forever."

"And ever."

EPILOGUE TWO

Millie

Three years later

"Alright, I'm calling it." Keiko flopped into the chair beside me. "We've officially lost control. The children are our rulers now."

I laughed, tipping my glass in her direction. "You're the one who said sugar was a great idea."

"Forgive me. I knew not what I was doing."

As if on cue, one of the nephews sprinted up to us, spraying us in the face with his water pistol before laughing manically and rushing away to join the rest of the tribe.

"Jesus," Keiko groaned, swiping at the water on her face. "Who in their right mind would want kids?"

I looked pointedly at her swollen belly. "Mm, who indeed?"

She waved me off. "Bloating, darling. It's all bloating."

"Uh-huh."

I searched the lawn, finding Ash in the midst of the wild-child pack, spray gun in one hand, our son clinging wildly to his back both laughing uproariously as they attempted to scramble out of the water-spray attack.

"Did they give you a date?" Keiko asked, pouring another glass of mocktail for herself.

"No." Nervous butterflies began to flitter in my stomach. "But they said it could be any day now."

After a lengthy process, we'd been approved as a foster family. Ash had been particularly passionate about giving kids the same opportunities his dad had given him growing up. We were now in the metaphorical waiting room, holding our breath for the phone call.

"You'll be awesome. But don't expect me to babysit." Keiko stood with a groan, her hands pressing into the small of her back. "These old bones weren't made for chasing kids."

I hid a smile. My friend was in deep, *deep* denial about her pregnancy. As she would say—there was a no vacancy sign on that uterus.

"See? There she is."

I turned to see my boys walking up the slight incline towards me, their bodies soaked, their expressions nearly identical grins.

Be still my heart.

Ash was the kind of father you wished everyone could have—hands-on, proactive, and willing to do whatever was necessary to give his kid the best life possible.

For a while, I'd fretted that our little munchkin might grow up to be an entitled dick—but Ash had settled those worries early on.

"Momma!"

I held out my arms, laughing when Ash plopped our wet baby in my lap. Xavier wrapped his arms around my neck, his chubby little fingers getting caught in my hair.

"You're all wet," I said, blowing raspberries on his neck, making him squeal.

"Wet!"

I looked up to see Ash pulling his cell out of his back pocket, his expression shifting as he hit answer.

"Hello?

I watched him over Xavier's head, letting my baby play with my hair.

"Yeah, of course. Now? Sure, we'll get the room ready. How old? Wow. Yeah. That's—of course. Thanks. Okay, bye."

He hung up staring at his phone for a moment then looked up, his gaze meeting mine.

"What?" I asked heart in my throat.

"That was CPS. They've got a little boy who needs a family. You interested?"

Goose bumps broke out along my skin; my gut knowing this little boy was going to be a part of our family.

"Absolutely."

Ash leaned in, laying a hand on Xavier's head.

"I love doing life with you, Millie."

I grinned, pressing a kiss to his lips. "Shall we do burgers for dinner?"

He laughed, holding out a hand to help me up, wrapping Xavier and me in his arms.

"Absolutely."

Thank you so much for reading Ash and Millie's story!
You can catch James' book in Pier Pressure.

You can continue the entire series by checking them out on my website at www.EvieMitchell.com

*If you enter the code **EBOOK10** you can get 10% off your purchase from my website.*

ABOUT THE AUTHOR

Hey, I'm Evie Mitchell.
I'm a thirty-something romance author
(she/her/hers) living with disability. I believe in
inclusion, accessibility, and fierce romance. My
loves include steamy romance novels, my sexy
husband, our THREE sausage dogs (THE
FUR!!!), and my ever-growing collection of
book-related mugs.

As a woman with a diverse work history,
including in areas such as hospitality, retail,
emergency response, event management,
human rights, disability access, and security—
my books are filled with true stories
(bridezillas), worst-case scenarios
(malfunctioning zippers), and my favorite
tropes (one-bed).

I'm a strong proponent of #OwnVoices, and
specialize in fiercely inclusive happily ever
afters.

EvieMitchell.com
Socials: @EvieMitchellAuthor

ALSO BY EVIE MITCHELL

All Access Series

Knot My Type

Love Flushed

Darn Knit All

Larsson Siblings

Thunder Thighs

Clean Sweep

The X-List

Reality Check

The Christmas Contract

The A-List

Capricorn Cove

The Shake-up

Double the D

Muffin Top

The Mrs. Clause

New Year, Knew You

Double Breasted

As You Wish

You Sleigh Me

Meat Load

Resolution Revolution

Dogg Pack

Puppy Love

Bad English

Pier Pressure

Trick or Trent

New Year's Faye

Reigning Hearts

The Marriage Claim

Silent Knight

Men of Trinity Bay

Kink in the Road

Nameless Souls MC

Runner

Wrath

Ghost

Shield

Elliot Security

Rough Edge
Bleeding Edge